Lineberger Memorial

Library

Lutheran Theological Southern Seminary   Columbia, S. C.

The Prince Mammoth Pumpkin

A Parable

James P. Adams

Illustrated by Julie Lonneman

PAULIST PRESS
New York, N.Y. • Mahwah, N.J.

Jacket design by Moe Berman

Text copyright © 1998 by James P. Adams; illustrations copyright © 1998 by Julie Lonneman

Library of Congress Cataloging-in-Publication Data

Adams, James P., 1965–
   The Prince Mammoth Pumpkin : a parable / James P. Adams ; illustrated by Julie Lonneman.
      p.   cm.
   ISBN 0-8091-0492-X (alk. paper)
   I. Lonneman, Julie, ill. II. Title.
PS3551.D3737P75   1998
813′.54—dc21   97-36879
                                                                                CIP

Published by Paulist Press
997 Macarthur Boulevard
Mahwah, New Jersey 07430

Printed and bound in the
United States of America

For Mary and the girls, of course,
and
in memory of a friend and mentor

Og Mandino
1923–1996

a storyteller, a man of faith, a man of love
and
in memory of two angelic boys,
Eric and Colin

All this Jesus said to the crowds in parables;
indeed he said nothing to them without a parable.
The Gospel of Matthew 13:34

The Farmer

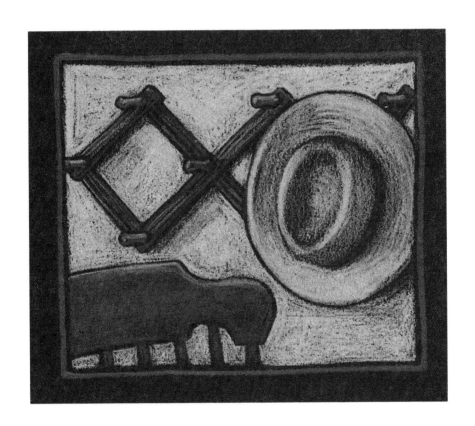

Three tall oak trees stood in a row at the top of the hill. At the bottom of the hill sat a cozy country cottage. The fertile stretch of land in-between was home to the most magnificent vegetable garden ever. The cottage was home to the farmer who worked that garden every day. He could remember when the oaks were barely tall enough to cast shadows and when the vegetable garden was just a hayfield.

The garden was the farmer's life. Early each spring he fertilized and tilled the soil on his old diesel tractor. Hot summer afternoons he spent pulling weeds between the rows of beans, running rabbits out of the lettuce patch and picking ripe, red tomatoes from the vine. From sunrise to sunset each day the farmer tended his garden.

The farmer raised potatoes, sweet corn, squash, carrots, peas, cucumbers—everything. He grew fifty times more than he could use. So all through the harvest season the farmer delivered baskets of sumptuous fresh vegetables to his neighbors. But he never knocked on their doors. He went out after nightfall and quietly left his offering on the front porch of each home. People wondered why the farmer kept his distance.

The farmer's favorite section of the garden was his pumpkin patch. The way he saw it, raising pumpkins was gardening in its truest, purest form. Most people raise gardens hoping to feast on delicious fresh vegetables all summer and not-so-bad canned vegetables through the winter. Pumpkins are different.

The only reason to raise pumpkins is for the sacred joy of it. At harvest time there is no reward on the dinner table for raising pumpkins. Instead, on Halloween morning, the best pumpkin in the patch is harvested and set out on the front porch for everyone to see. When evening comes, one of the children trick or treating, or a parent waiting at the edge of the yard, might call out, "Hey, nice pumpkin!"

And you can say, "Thanks, I grew it myself." That's it. That's the only reward for growing pumpkins.

During the cold and snow of winter, the short days and long nights were lonely for the farmer. He had no earth to till, no plants to tend, no harvest to bring in. He was alone. In the winter it was hard to fight back the bitter chill of memories. The farmer's wife, whom he loved so much, had died too young. Had it been twenty years or two weeks? It was all the same to him...an open wound. So he kept his distance.

Through the dark winter months the farmer passed his time sitting beside his fireplace with gardening magazines and seed catalogues. And so it was on one February evening when he came upon an article about a young man in another part of the country who had developed a new variety of pumpkin called The Prince Mammoth Pumpkin. The article said that each plant would produce just one pumpkin and that a package of seeds sold for twenty-eight dollars.

The farmer was irritated. "I'd plow my garden under before I'd pay twenty-eight dollars for a package of pumpkin seeds!" he grumbled. Then he glanced at the opposite page and saw the picture: It was a photograph of the young man who had developed and named the new variety, along with his smiling, eight-year-old son. Between them was a genuine, full-grown The Prince Mammoth Pumpkin. The farmer was amazed. The pumpkin was bigger than the boy.

The next morning the farmer was waiting at the door of the bank when it opened. He withdrew twenty-eight dollars from his savings account and mailed it to The Prince Mammoth Pumpkin Company for one package of pumpkin seeds.

The Planting

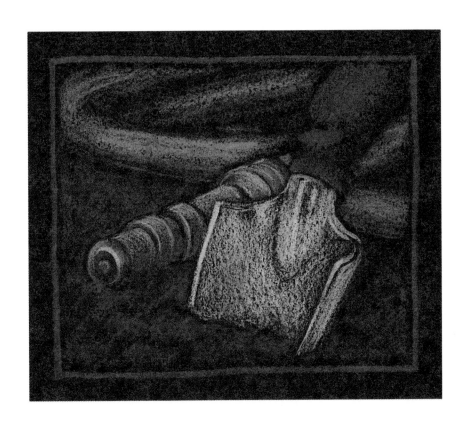

Two weeks later his package arrived. The farmer tore it open like a child opening a present on Christmas morning. Inside the gray envelope he found a catalogue, special planting instructions and a small seed envelope. Afraid he might spill the seeds, the farmer opened the envelope carefully and emptied the contents into the palm of his hand. He looked with disbelief at one, solitary pumpkin seed.

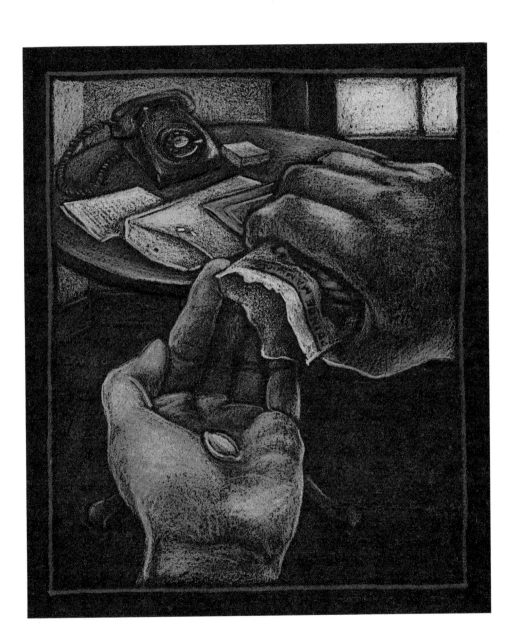

The farmer was furious. "I'll plow my garden under before I'll pay twenty-eight dollars for one pumpkin seed!" he shouted as he picked up the phone to call the company. He was determined to get his money back. He dialed the number on the cover of the catalogue. As the phone was ringing, he flipped through the pages of the catalogue. "Twenty-eight dollars for one pumpkin seed. What do they think, I'm stupid?" Then, there in the catalogue, he spotted a familiar photograph. It showed the young man, his smiling son and that real, full-grown Prince Mammoth Pumpkin. "Amazing," the farmer whispered to himself. The pumpkin was bigger than the boy.

A woman answered the phone. "Good morning," she said. "Prince Mammoth Pumpkin Company. May I help you?"

The farmer froze. "No...I don't think so," he said. "I guess I must have dialed the wrong number." He hung up the phone. He had to have that pumpkin.

When spring finally arrived the farmer planted his twenty-eight-dollar pumpkin seed in the rich soil at the top of the hill, in the shadow of the oak trees. Before long the seed sprouted a single leaf and, eventually, a tiny yellow flower. Within a month the bud gave way to a bouncing baby Prince Mammoth Pumpkin. The farmer was pleased.

In the course of tending the rest of his garden, the farmer checked on "the Prince," as he called it, at least three times every day. He worried about it and cared for it as if it were his only child. The Prince responded to the farmer's love and care. Its thick, curving ribs were taking form. The Prince's skin was growing toward a deeper, richer orange in the summer sun. It was all that the farmer hoped it would be. As the Prince grew, so did the farmer's joy.

By late October the Prince had grown so large that the farmer could see it from the front porch of his cottage. On the afternoon before Halloween, when the sun was low in the sky, the farmer looked up at the Prince with pride as it leaned against the center oak tree. In the morning he would drive the tractor to the top of the hill, load the Prince on his wagon, haul it down and set it out on the front porch before the trick-or-treating started. The farmer was excited. "God is so good," he thought.

The Plowing

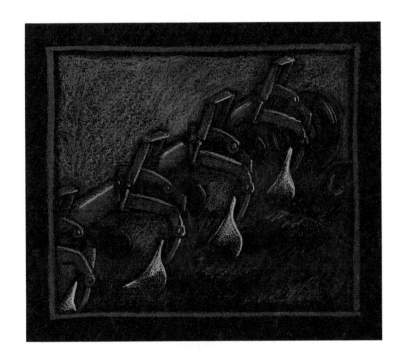

T hrough the light rain on Halloween morning the farmer drove up the dirt pathway to the top of the hill. His wagon rattled along behind the tractor. This was the day for which he had worked so hard. He could only imagine how the neighborhood children were going to react to his splendid pumpkin. But when the farmer reached the top of the hill he knew something was wrong. His eyes searched the scene. He didn't see the Prince. A large axe was impaled in the center oak tree.

His gaze turned to the ground, and suddenly he realized what had happened. The Prince had been destroyed. Vandals had come during the night and hacked it into pieces. The life of the Prince had been poured out on the hillside.

The rain was now coming down hard. The farmer didn't notice. "How could they do this? Why did it happen? What am I supposed to do now?" His shock turned to rage. He knew what to do. No one was going to get anything from his garden ever again.

He turned the tractor around, lowered the tiller blades and proceeded to plow under the entire garden. He revved the old diesel engine and plowed under row after row: Down went the tomatoes, down went the string beans, down went the sweet corn and peas. His rage lasted three hours.

When it was finished every crop had been destroyed. The farmer stood in the driving rain at the foot of the center oak tree. He wept like a parent for the death of a child. He wept for the evil in the human heart. He wept for the evil buried in his own heart. He wept for God who seemed so distant. He wept for his childhood dreams that had faded away. He wept for the loss of love and the emptiness of his lonely life. He wept for all his failures and disappointments, for the places to which he had never traveled and for the person he might have become. He wept for his own destructive anger and for the loss of his beloved garden and for the Prince, now dead and buried.

Despite the hard rain that lasted all Halloween day and night, children trudged up to the farmer's unlit, unpumpkined front porch. They came dressed as clowns, witches, dinosaurs and other strange creatures to knock on the farmer's door hoping for a Halloween treat. But the farmer did not answer the door. He sat in the shadows of his darkened living room and stared out at the rain, at the disappointed children in their costumes and at parents waiting for them at the edge of the yard. The farmer was dead inside.

One little boy was more persistent than the other children. He was an angel. He knocked on the farmer's door, waited, and knocked again. The farmer did not answer. The boy peered through his winged reflection on the dark window. He saw the grieving farmer sitting in the shadows. For a moment their eyes met. The boy's heart went out to him. He knocked on the door a third time, but still the farmer did not answer. Finally the boy went on to the next house.

Two weeks later the farmer closed up the cottage and left town. No one knew where he went. The plowed-under garden was a mystery to everyone.

The Garden

A year later a group of children were playing base-ball in a field beside the farmer's long driveway when they saw a man who looked like the farmer, but older, drive up in a flatbed truck. It was the farmer. He had sold his trac-tor to a family in the next county, and he had come to fetch it for them. The farmer climbed from the truck and headed for the front porch of the cottage. The children watched with curiosity.

One boy stepped forward. "Excuse me, sir," he said shyly. "My mom says that if you say it's okay, I can have one of your pumpkins. Do you think I could?"

The farmer responded slowly, "Son, I don't have any pumpkins."

"Oh yes, sir. You do. Come and see. You have a bunch!"

The boy took the farmer by the hand and led him up the porch steps. The farmer gazed down on the boy, sorry to disappoint him. The boy turned his head to meet the farmer's glance. "Don't be afraid," his eyes seemed to say. Suddenly the farmer remembered the boy's angelic face and tears filled his eyes. "Sir, why are you crying?" asked the boy. "Look what has become of your garden."

The farmer raised his head. He could hardly believe his eyes. When he plowed under his garden in the rain, he had also plowed under the remains of the Prince. The plowing and the rain had spread hundreds of Prince Mammoth Pumpkin seeds through the whole garden. The farmer stared over his land. Before him was a field full of big, beautiful Prince Mammoth Pumpkins.

"Yes," he said. "Yes, you can have one of my pumpkins. You and every one of your friends."

As the children streamed into the garden, the farmer wept for joy. He wept for the little boy who had reunited him with his beloved garden. He wept for the power that redeems what is evil in the human heart. He wept for the miracle of new and abundant life and love, and for the beauty of his reborn garden. He wept for the love of God who makes all things new. He wept for the mighty resurrection of the Prince.

The first knock on the door came at six o'clock. The farmer opened the door with a basket of candy in his hand. On the front porch stood two children holding hands, brother and sister, one dressed as a black cat, the other as a white cat. They were standing beside the Prince. The farmer smiled. The pumpkin was bigger than the children!

The farmer looked to the edge of the yard where their parents waited. The father had something to say: "Hey, nice pumpkin. Did you grow it yourself?"

The farmer answered him slowly. "No. No, I did not grow it myself. It was a gift."

And he thought to himself: "God is so good."